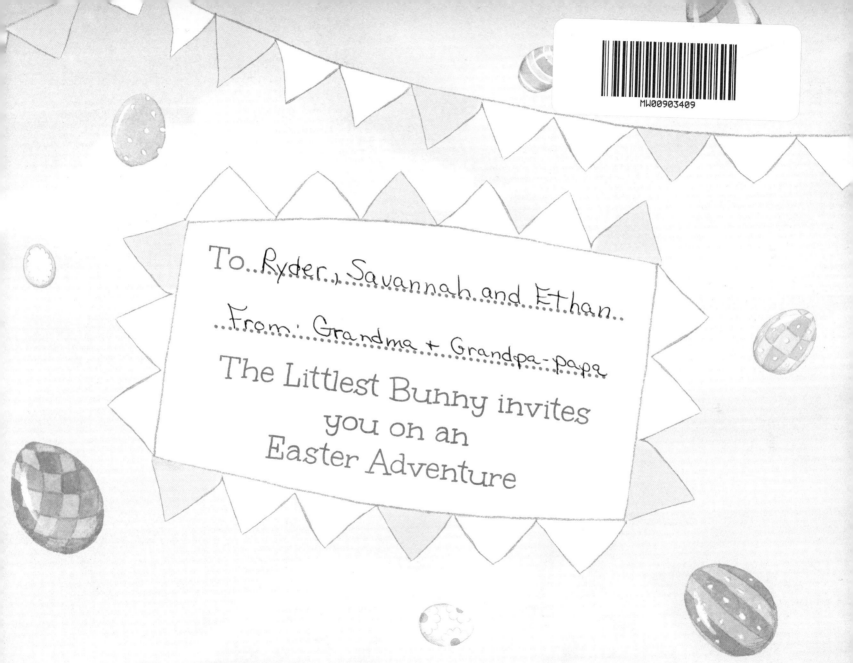

To..Ryder.,.Savannah.and..Ethan..

..From.:.Grandma.+.Grandpa-papa

The Littlest Bunny invites
you on an
Easter Adventure

an Easter Adventure

The Littlest Bunny in Iowa

Written by Lily Jacobs
Illustrated by Robert Dunn and Stefano Azzalin
Designed by Sarah Allen

Published by Sourcebooks Jabberwocky, an imprint of Sourcebooks, Inc.
P.O. Box 4410, Naperville, Illinois 60567-4410
(630) 961-3900
Fax: (630) 961-2168
www.jabberwockykids.com

Library of Congress Cataloging-in-Publication data is on file with the publisher.

Date of Production: September 2015
Run Number: HTW_PO100815
Printed and bound in China
10 9 8 7 6 5 4 3 2

an Easter Adventure

The Littlest Bunny in Iowa

Written by Lily Jacobs
Illustrated by Robert Dunn

sourcebooks
jabberwocky

Not long ago, in a land you might know,
Lived a girl named May and a boy named Joe.

WELCOME TO IOWA

They were moving to Iowa, and longed to explore,
Make new friends, have adventures, and many things more!

Iowa Pet Store

On the day before Easter,
they rode into town.
They went to the pet store
and looked all around.

There in the front
was a pen full of bunnies.
The small ones were cute,
and the big ones were funny.

They played with the bunnies
and thought for a bit,
And then they agreed
on the most *perfect* fit:

The *littlest* bunny,
with the sweetest small hop.

"He's ours!" May announced.
"Let's call him Flop."

So Flop joined the family
that sunny spring day.
The littlest bunny
was now home to stay.

They played with the bunny until it was late,
Then settled Flop into his cozy, snug crate.

May gave Flop a kiss
and Joe patted his head.
And then the two children
both climbed into bed.

A soft evening breeze blew in through the window,
And May and Joe smiled as they slept on their pillows.

But Flop had no time now
to close his own eyes:
He was preparing
an Easter surprise!

He was quite little,
that much was true,
But tonight our dear Flop
had a big job to do.

For he had a secret
he hadn't let show:

He was the Easter Bunny, and he had to go!

A magical wind gave his whiskers a tickle.
His nose, how it twitched! His ears, how they wiggled!

Soon, Flop was quite different than ever before,
And he couldn't wait—not for one moment more!

He raced through the house and out into the night,
To where he had hidden his eggs out of sight.

Map of Iowa

His marvelous burrow held Easter eggs plenty:
To be quite exact, **nine million and twenty!**
He packed up the eggs; he looked at the map.
He fastened his goggles and his red flying cap.

Then Flop hopped right into
his hot air balloon,
And soon he was soaring
as high as the moon!

As he watched his first stop grow nearer and nearer, His **Hawkeye State mission** became even clearer.

First, Flop balanced eggs
on a tall building top...

...Then he went to
the park, spreading
eggs as he hopped.

And then he dashed off
for an **Easter home run**...

...Then quietly hid
chocolate eggs, one by one.

With big bounces here and giant jumps there,

Flop hid Iowa's eggs everywhere!

WEST   EAST

He flew to the **east**, to the **south**,
west, and **north**.
He crisscrossed the state; he raced
back and **forth**.

Dubuque and Des Moines and Sioux City got treats.
Then Iowa City and Davenport too were complete.

Ames, Cedar Rapids—the long list went on.
Flop was delivering his eggs until dawn!

Finally, Flop found his very last stop.
He came to *your* house with a bounce and a hop!
And there he delivered his Easter surprises:
So many eggs, of all shapes and sizes!
And when he was done,
he stopped for a rest.

Yes, surely this Easter
was one of his best!

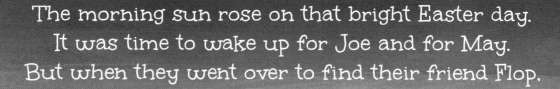

The morning sun rose on that bright Easter day.
It was time to wake up for Joe and for May.
But when they went over to find their friend Flop,

The door was wide open—
his crate was unlocked!

There were eggs to discover, as all children know.
"But we just want Flop!" cried May and cried Joe.

They looked under their beds; they looked all around.
But the littlest bunny just couldn't be found.

Then from 'round the corner came a faint *tap-tap-tap*.
They rushed and they stumbled. It had to be him!
And there they found baskets—
and something else was tucked in?

"It's Flop!" they cried out, and held him so close.
Joe tickled his ears and May kissed his pink nose.
Flop hugged them back, his new friends so dear.

Happy Easter to Iowa!
See you next year!

Did you find all the Easter eggs
hidden in Iowa?
Look back through the book to see
if you can spot all 20 eggs.

Give up?
Check the answers
on the last page.

Did you find them all?